SPEED RACER™

The Secret Engine

GROSSET & DUNLAP
Published by the Penguin Group
Penguin Group (USA) Inc., 375 Hudson Street,
New York, New York 10014, USA
Penguin Group (Canada), 90 Eglinton Avenue East, Suite 700,
Toronto, Ontario M4P 2Y3, Canada
(a division of Pearson Penguin Canada Inc.)
Penguin Books Ltd., 80 Strand,
London WC2R 0RL, England
Penguin Group Ireland, 25 St. Stephen's Green,
Dublin 2, Ireland
(a division of Penguin Books Ltd.)
Penguin Group (Australia), 250 Camberwell Road, Camberwell,
Victoria 3124, Australia
(a division of Pearson Australia Group Pty. Ltd.)
Penguin Books India Pvt. Ltd., 11 Community Centre,
Panchsheel Park, New Delhi—110 017, India
Penguin Group (NZ), 67 Apollo Drive,
Rosedale, North Shore 0632, New Zealand
(a division of Pearson New Zealand Ltd.)
Penguin Books (South Africa) (Pty.) Ltd., 24 Sturdee Avenue,
Rosebank, Johannesburg 2196, South Africa

Penguin Books Ltd., Registered Offices: 80 Strand, London WC2R 0RL, England

www.speedracer.com

Library of Congress Cataloging-in-Publication Data is available.

ISBN 978-0-448-44806-0   10 9 8 7 6 5 4 3 2 1

SPEED RACER™

The Secret Engine

by Chase Wheeler   Grosset & Dunlap

The Marvels of the Mach 5

The Mach 5 is one of the most
powerful and amazing racing cars in
the world. Pops Racer designed the Mach 5
with features you won't see on any other car.
All of the features can be controlled by
buttons on the steering wheel.

This button releases powerful jacks to boost the car so Sparky, the mechanic, can quickly make any necessary repairs or adjustments.

Press this button and the Mach 5 sprouts special grip tires for traction over any terrain. At the same time, an incredible 5,000 torque of horsepower is distributed equally to each wheel by auxiliary engines.

For use when Speed Racer has to race over heavily wooded terrain, powerful rotary saws protrude from the front of the Mach 5 to slash and cut any and all obstacles.

Pressing the D button releases a powerful deflector that seals the cockpit into an air-conditioned, crash and bulletproof, watertight chamber. Inside it, Speed Racer is completely isolated and shielded.

The button for special illumination allows Speed Racer to see much farther and more clearly than with ordinary headlights. It's invaluable in some of the weird and dangerous places he races the Mach 5.

Press this button when the Mach 5 is underwater. First the cockpit is supplied with oxygen, then a periscope is raised to scan the surface of the water. Everything that is seen is relayed down to the cockpit by television.

This releases a homing robot from the front of the car. The homing robot can carry pictures or tape-recorded messages to anyone or anywhere Speed Racer wants.

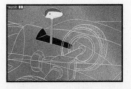

The Mach 5 hugged the tight curves of the mountain, whipping fast around the roadway that lined the cliff. Speed Racer was behind the wheel, loving every second of the wild ride.

Speed's goal in life was to become a professional race car driver, and right now he was in training for the Multipeak Race. It cost a lot of money to enter the Multipeak Race, but Speed wasn't worried about getting the money—he'd find a way. Speed's dad, Pops Racer, was the

automobile engineer who had designed this sleek white race car called the Mach 5. It was like no other race car ever built. Not only could the car take these swift mountain turns with ease, it was also made with special gadgets so it could withstand any obstacle thrown at it.

Just that morning Pops had given the Mach 5 a tune-up. Now Speed was taking it for a high-powered test drive with the radio on and the convertible top down.

In the passenger seat were Speed's little brother, Spritle, and his pet chimpanzee, Chim Chim. They had begged to come along for the ride, but now they were fighting over a banana. Spritle refused to share.

Just then, it began to rain. Speed pushed a button on the steering wheel, and the cockpit slid shut. The music stopped with a breaking news bulletin. A prisoner had escaped from Songalong Prison!

"The fugitive is the notorious Tongue

Blaggard," the radio announcer said. "He is said to be hiding in or around Hightaxtown."

"Eeee!" shrieked Spritle.

Chim Chim hooted with worry.

Hightaxtown was close by.

"Be careful," the radio announcer continued. "This man is dangerous."

Speed was about to say not to worry when he noticed another car coming around the bend. It was an antique Model T. Speed couldn't remember the last time he saw one of those old cars on the road. He didn't even know people drove them anymore!

Just as they came close, the Model T pulled to a stop. The top was down, and rain poured into the car.

Speed stopped the Mach 5 beside it.

"Some car," said Sprite. "Who'd want to drive an old piece of junk like that?"

But Sprite had said that too loudly. The driver of the Model T, a cranky old man, had heard him.

"This car is not junk!" the old man shouted into the rain.

Sitting in the Model T beside the old man was a teenage girl. "You tell him, Grandpa!" she yelled.

Speed leaned out the window so the old man could hear him through the rain. "Keep your eyes on the road ahead," Speed called. He pointed at the twisting road that led farther up the mountain. "With this rain, it could be dangerous."

"Young man," the old man snapped, "how

am I supposed to keep my eyes on the road? I can't even *see* the road with this rain."

"Why not roll the top closed?" Speed suggested.

"Why don't you mind your own business?" the old man said.

The rain was coming down in sheets. With the top of the Model T down, the old man and his granddaughter were drenched.

The old man got out of the Model T. He slammed the door and started closing the rolltop.

"Can I help?" Speed offered.

"Do I look like I need help?" the old man shouted.

Speed *did* think the old man looked like he needed help—but he didn't want to be rude. Still, he couldn't help but admire the old man's antique car. "What a car!" he said. "A hand crank . . . wooden spoke wheels . . . a vertical windshield . . ."

The old man got angry. He pointed at the Mach 5. "Just take that junk heap of yours and drive away."

The Mach 5 was definitely no junk heap. And besides, Speed would not just drive away. He couldn't leave them alone in the rain. Since the old man didn't want his help, Speed waited patiently until the old man was done closing the top.

Many minutes later, the top of the Model T was finally closed. The stubborn old man had done the work himself. "There," he said, panting. "I did it." He wiped sweat from his brow.

"But now it's stopped raining," Spritle called out.

That was true: The sky had cleared, and now the sun was coming out.

The old man looked up at the sky. "But I spent all that time putting that top up! I wish it would keep raining."

"I'm sorry," Speed said.

Then Speed turned and chuckled to himself.

Seeing that, Spritle started to laugh. Chim Chim joined in. Even the old man's granddaughter, sitting inside the Model T, started to laugh. She tried to cover her mouth so her grandfather wouldn't see.

The old man was not amused.

"Stop laughing!" he demanded. "I'm an old man! It's not funny!"

"It's not very polite to laugh at my grandfather," his granddaughter added. "Shame on you."

"She was laughing," Spritle protested to

Speed, pointing at the granddaughter. "Come on, Speed. Let's get out of here."

Speed hopped back in the Mach 5.

Before he left, he called out to the old man, "We heard a report on the radio. An escaped convict is in the area. You'd better be careful."

The old man made a face. "Thanks for the warning, but an escaped convict doesn't scare *me*."

Speed shrugged. The old man just wasn't very friendly. He hit the gas, and the Mach 5 sped away.

Spritle peeked out the window at the old man and his granddaughter in the distance. "I hope they'll be okay," he said.

Later, Speed—along with other drivers looking to compete in the Multipeak Race—was at the racetrack. He was in his car practicing the finer points of driving under the instruction of Fireball Rust, one of the greatest racers of all time.

"Good work, Speed. You took advantage of that straightaway," Fireball announced over the racetrack's loudspeaker. "Now get ready for that curve up ahead. Be sure to shift down, and then when you pull out of it, open wide!"

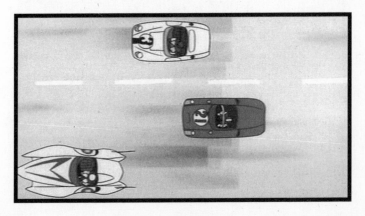

Speed did exactly what Fireball told him to do, and the Mach 5 made it around the curve perfectly.

"Go, Speed, go!" Spritle cheered from beside the track.

Chim Chim cheered for Speed, too. He jumped up and down, clapping and hooting.

After the initial laps, Fireball joined Speed in the Mach 5 for some one-on-one instruction.

"From now on, I want you to only use your heel and toe on the pedals," Fireball instructed.

"Okay," Speed replied.

"Now, Speed, give it the gun!" Fireball said.

"Here goes . . . ," said Speed.

Speed stepped down hard on the accelerator and launched the Mach 5 forward. Gripping the steering wheel tightly, Speed raced the Mach 5 along the straightaway.

"You're coming to a curve. Now get ready to use the brake," Fireball said.

Reacting too quickly, Speed immediately pressed his toe down onto the brake. The Mach 5 skidded toward the wall.

"You hit the brake too soon!" Fireball shouted.

"Sorry," Speed mumbled.

"Now use the clutch. Okay, release the clutch and give it gas. More gas! The engine's not running fast enough! Check the tachometer! Don't use the brake so much! For curves like this, shift to second and let the engine do some of the slowing down!" Fireball barked out the instructions without taking a breath.

Speed glanced at the tachometer, the instrument that kept track of how fast his engine was running. If the number got too high, it meant his engine was going too fast and heating up!

Quickly reacting to each one of Fireball's orders, Speed maneuvered the Mach 5 around the curve, skidding a little, but getting past the turn safely even at such a high speed.

Beads of sweat ran down Speed's forehead. That was a close one!

After the individual instruction, Fireball had the drivers stand far away from their cars in a line at the edge of the track. It was time to move on to the next lesson of the day.

"All right. Now we're going to practice doing a running start to your cars," Fireball announced. "Speed, you're first. Show us how fast you can get your car started."

"Yes, sir," said Speed. He lowered the visor on his racing helmet, shook out his legs, and got into position.

"Go!" Fireball barked.

Speed took off running toward the Mach 5.

"Faster, Speed! Pick it up!" Fireball shouted.

Speed was running as fast as he could, but he tried to go even faster. That's when he tripped and fell face-first onto the track.

"Ugh!" exclaimed Speed as his chest hit the asphalt.

The other drivers laughed.

"On your feet!" Fireball shouted.

Speed stood up, took a breath, and then continued his sprint toward the Mach 5.

When he reached the Mach 5, Speed pressed his hands onto the door and vaulted himself into the air, hoping to land directly in the driver's seat. Unfortunately, he overshot his mark and flew past the car entirely! He landed with a thud outside the car.

"Oof!" Speed groaned.

The other drivers were laughing even louder than before.

"Do it over!" shouted Fireball.

As Speed got back to his feet, he noticed a masked man standing high atop the racetrack's wall. On closer inspection Speed recognized that the man was Racer X, the best racer on the circuit!

Unknown to Speed, Racer X was his older brother, Rex, who had run away from home years ago to pursue his dream of becoming a professional race car driver.

Like an expert acrobat, Racer X flipped down from the high wall and landed on both feet. Then he sprinted toward the Mach 5 at incredible speed.

"Whoa! Look at him go!" one of the other drivers gasped.

"Nobody's as fast as Racer X," another driver added.

Racer X quickly reached the Mach 5, vaulted over the door right into the driver's seat, instantly started the engine, and took off!

Racer X sped down the track in the Mach 5 at top speed. His expert driving skills wowed everyone, and he completed a lap around the entire track in record time.

"That's the way it should be done," Fireball said. "Nobody can get off to a faster start and maintain top speed as well as Racer X."

Racer X pulled the Mach 5 to a stop alongside his own yellow racing car. It had the number 9 on the doors.

Racer X hopped out of the Mach 5, did a forward flip into his own car, and sped away as quickly as he'd appeared.

"Wow! That's fast!" said Speed.

"Nobody in the world can beat Racer X," said one of the other drivers.

"Well, I'm going to try my best to be the fastest," vowed Speed. "Maybe I'll have the chance to race against Racer X in the Multipeak Race. Then we'll see."

After practice, Speed, Spritle, and Chim Chim drove in the Mach 5 along the same mountain road they'd traveled earlier that day. They saw a shape in the distance.

"Look who's up ahead," Speed observed.

Stopped in the road was the Model T. The old man and his granddaughter were kneeling down by one of the tires.

Speed slowed the Mach 5 to a stop beside the Model T.

"You must have a flat tire," Speed said. "Don't worry, I'll change it for you." He hopped out of his car, ready to help.

"Here comes that nosy boy again to bother us," the old man muttered.

Speed tried to ignore him.

"Go away!" the old man shouted. "I don't like

anybody who drives those newfangled automatic cars like yours, young man! You don't appreciate the pleasure of driving with a stick shift and a real honest-to-goodness clutch!"

"But my car *does* have a stick shift, sir," Speed said.

"Huh?!" the old man exclaimed. He approached the Mach 5 to see for himself. "Hmm. Not bad," he admitted.

"After I help fix your tire, sir, would you like a ride in the Mach 5?" Speed asked.

The old man smiled for the first time. "Why, thank you, young man. I'd love to," he replied.

Soon after, the Model T's flat tire was fixed, and everyone was out for a ride. Speed and the old man were in the Mach 5, and the old man's granddaughter, Spritle, and Chim Chim followed in the Model T.

"So . . . what do you think of the Mach 5?" Speed asked the old man as they whipped around a turn.

The old man inspected the car's interior. "I'd like you to explain what these buttons are on the steering column," he said.

"Well, each one controls a special feature. Anything from jumping over obstacles to driving underwater," Speed explained. "They were designed and built by my father," he added proudly.

"This is a fabulous car, young man. I must confess . . . I like it," the old man said at last.

Speed grinned. He knew the old man would come around. Who couldn't like the Mach 5?

To thank Speed for fixing his tire and for giving him an exciting ride in the Mach 5, the old man invited them all back to his house for dinner. He had a large house in the mountains. Inside, everyone was seated around a vast dining table set with huge amounts of food. Aside from Spritle and the old man's teenage granddaughter, there were ten other children at the table. Speed was surprised to learn that the old man had so many kids.

"Do all the children here belong to you, sir?" Spritle asked.

"Yes, I adopted every one of them except, of course, for my granddaughter, Susie," the old man answered. "Each of these children needed a home, and I provided it." The children smiled at him with affection.

"That's very kind of you, sir," Speed said. "There should be more people in the world like you."

"I'd like to give them a better home, but I don't make much money as a taxicab washer," the old man lamented.

"Oh," Speed said sadly.

"Someday, I'll do better for them," the old man said quietly.

Speed wished he could do something to help.

◎　◎　◎　◎

Meanwhile, very close by, a mean-looking man and his driver were prowling the dark mountain roads in a large black car. They listened intently to a news bulletin on the radio.

"The whereabouts of the escaped convict Blaggard are still unknown at this hour. Police are on high alert," the radio announcer said.

The mean-looking man turned off the radio and roared in laughter. His dark, heavy brows lifted, and his bald head gleamed in the dark night.

"Those cops are wasting their time," he growled. "They'll never catch *me*. I'm out of jail forever." He was the infamous Tongue Blaggard, the criminal the police were searching for. He

snickered with obvious delight.

The car came to a screeching halt. Blaggard's driver had noticed something.

"Hey, Mr. Blaggard, there it is—a Model T," the driver said.

The headlights of Blaggard's car shone brightly on the Model T parked in the driveway of the old man's house.

"That one looks just like the car owned by Light Fingers Clepto," Blaggard said. "C'mon. Let's get it."

After dinner, the old man walked Speed, Spritle, and Chim Chim to the door. "If you drive the Mach 5 in the Multipeak Race, I'm sure you'll win, Speed," the old man was saying.

"Thank you, sir," said Speed. "I hope to be able to save enough money to enter that race. And if I'm in it, I'll try my best to win!"

"You can do it, Speed!" Susie assured him.

They stepped out into the dark driveway.

"Oh, no! The Model T!" cried Spritle.

Everyone looked to the spot in the driveway where the Model T had been parked just before dinner. It was empty.

"It's gone!" the old man shouted in disbelief.

"Somebody must have stolen it, Grandpa," Susie said quietly.

"This is terrible!" the old man cried. "That was our only means of transportation! For me, my granddaughter, and all the children! I don't have the money to buy a new car!" He stood in the empty spot, holding his head in his hands.

"I'm so sorry, sir," Speed said. He glanced at the Mach 5, parked in the driveway undisturbed. It was odd that someone had stolen the old car but not the Mach 5.

"That car was left to me by Light Fingers Clepto!" the old man cried.

Speed looked startled. "You didn't say . . .
Light Fingers Clepto?"

"The famous crook?" Spritle added.

Speed had heard stories about Light Fingers
Clepto; everyone had. He was a notorious thief
who had been killed many decades earlier. Speed
hadn't expected this kind old man to know such
an infamous criminal.

"Yes," the old man said. He took a step closer
to Speed, wanting to explain himself. "You see,
Speed . . . Light Fingers Clepto was my father."

Speed didn't know what to say.

The old man—Mr. Clepto—told Speed how his father had been double-crossed by his own men over forty-five years ago. It was on his deathbed that he told his son about the car, his beloved Model T. "Just before it was all over, he called me to his bedside and said, 'The car,'" Mr. Clepto said. "Those were his last words."

"I'm so very sorry," Speed said.

"He was bad. A first-class crook, but I loved him. He was my father," the old man continued. "After that I had nothing but trouble and bad luck. I was poor, but no matter how poor I became, I hung on to that car because I knew it was what my father wanted me to do. It was my monument to him."

"Don't worry. I'll get it back to you," Speed assured him.

"And I'll help my brother," Spritle added.

"Do your best, Speed," the old man said.

"I shall," Speed said.

It was the next morning at Pops's Motors, the new garage and automotive factory Pops had opened, and Pops and his mechanic, Sparky, were sitting around doing absolutely nothing.

"There hasn't been a single customer since we opened the factory, and I make the best engines and cars in the world!" Pops cried, raising his fist in the air.

"Maybe that's the problem, Pops," Sparky said. "Maybe people just don't appreciate a car that's really top-notch."

"If business doesn't get better, we won't even have enough money to send Speed to the Multipeak Race," Pops lamented.

Mom Racer entered the garage with a plate of cookies.

"Cheer up, the both of you," she said. "I'm

sure you'll have lots of customers very soon."

"I fear we might have to go out of business," Pops said gloomily.

Sparky took a tiny nibble of a cookie and nodded sadly.

"Think of all the things we can be grateful for," Mom said. "You have a wonderful factory and garage. Speed and Spritle are two fine sons. All we need to make life really perfect is for Rex to come home."

"Our oldest son was foolish to run away from home," Pops said.

They ate their cookies in silence.

They didn't know it, but someone was listening in on this conversation, someone they never would have guessed.

It was Racer X. He was standing just outside the garage, hidden in the shadows.

With his mask on, not even his own parents would have known he was really Rex Racer.

Maybe I was foolish to run away, Pops, Racer X thought. *And someday I will come back, but right now, as Racer X, I'll make sure that my brother Speed becomes the best racer in the world.*

With that, he leaped into his yellow car and gunned the engine.

Inside the garage, Pops, Mom, and Sparky heard a car peel out. They rushed outside, thinking it might be a customer, but it was too late.

Whoever it was had driven away.

Trixie, Speed's girlfriend, was flying in her helicopter high over the mountains on the lookout for the stolen Model T. Trixie could always be counted on to help Speed whenever he was in a bind.

She scanned the area far below. Then she

saw, off a dirt road at the bottom of a ravine, what looked like an old car. It was flipped on its side, its hood gaping open.

"Oh!" Trixie exclaimed. She radioed to Speed. "Trixie, calling the Mach 5."

Over the radio she heard: "This is the Mach 5. Trixie, come in."

"I've found the Model T!" Trixie replied. "It's off Highway Eight, near the bridge on the River Quinn." She began lowering the helicopter to make a landing.

"I'll be there as fast as I can," Speed said. He made a U-turn in the Mach 5 and started for the River Quinn.

5 ENGINE TROUBLE

There hadn't been a customer at Pops's Motors all day. Pops and Sparky had fallen asleep on a stack of crates, snoring away.

Speed and Trixie burst into the garage. The noise startled Pops and Sparky, who both woke up, looking around wildly.

"It must be a customer!" Sparky cried.

"What can we do for you?!" Pops added, rubbing his eyes blearily.

Then, when they saw that it was only Speed and Trixie, they frowned.

"It's only you two," Pops grumbled. "I thought business was picking up."

Trixie and Speed exchanged a look. They had an idea . . . they just needed Pops to go along with it.

Trixie shot Pops a bright smile. "You know,

Pops, maybe business will pick up. *If* you do some promotional work, people around town will start talking about you. . . "

"Promotional work?!" Pops said. "I already have an ad in the paper."

"You've got to show people you're willing to work below cost," Trixie said.

"Huh," Pops said, not yet convinced. "How can I?"

"For your first customer," Speed said, stealing a glance at Trixie, "don't charge anything at all."

"Don't charge anything at all?!" Pops said, shocked.

"If you're really dedicated to your business,

you shouldn't think about money," Trixie said.

Pops looked down at his shoes. It was true—having his own garage was a dream come true. He'd do anything to make it work.

"Okay," Pops said. "You know what? It'll be free . . . to the first customer!"

At that, Speed and Trixie broke into giant grins. Their plan had worked. They turned to look outside the garage, where Mr. Clepto and Susie were standing before their antique Model T. Speed had gotten the Model T towed to Pops's garage.

"C'mon in, Mr. Clepto!" Trixie cried. "It's all arranged!"

Not minutes later, Sparky had the hood of the Model T propped open and was poking his head inside to have a look. The car's engine was broken, but Sparky could repair any automobile, no matter what the damage. Still, he'd never worked on such an old car before.

Mr. Clepto stood beside his Model T with

pride. "Well, what do you think?" he asked Sparky. He sounded so hopeful.

Sparky was about to warn Mr. Clepto that he might not have the experience to fix an antique engine like this when he noticed something. That engine was no antique!

"Did you know that you have a brand-new engine in this old, uh, I mean, *antique* car, sir?" Sparky asked.

"Oh, sure," Mr. Clepto said. "The old engine's in the attic."

Sparky looked confused.

Susie stepped up to explain. "The original

engine broke down on us," she said. "So Grandpa had it replaced with this new one here. It was cheaper than buying a whole new car, you see. But we couldn't just throw away the old engine—"

"My father built up that old engine before he died," Mr. Clepto interrupted gruffly. "He loved this car."

"I see," said Pops, and he did. He understood hanging on to old broken-down machinery for purely sentimental reasons. Cars were more than transportation from place to place for Pops—they were the most amazing things he'd ever seen.

Mr. Clepto quickly changed the subject. "So can you fix it or not?"

"Well, sure," Sparky said. "It's funny, but it looks like your engine was tampered with."

Pops leaned in to have a closer look. He nodded. "Looks like someone took out your engine, sir, and then tried to put it back."

"Whoever it was sure didn't know what they

were doing," Sparky added. "Your carburetor wasn't connected right. These hoses are all mixed up." In seconds, Sparky reattached the carburetor, and the engine started up just like new.

Susie cheered.

There was a sudden commotion outside.

Some cars had pulled up in front of Pops's Motors. Oddly enough, they were all also antique Model Ts. The drivers jumped out.

"Fix my car!" one yelled.

"My car's next!" another yelled.

Pops looked about to keel over. Suddenly, he had many customers!

Trixie winked at Speed. "Looks like our little idea worked," she said.

"But do all the customers have to have Model Ts?" said Pops. He threw up his hands in good-natured frustration. "Those old cars sure take a lot of work."

Speed agreed that it was odd. And odder still was when Sparky had a look under all of the Model Ts' hoods and discovered that they all had similar problems. It seemed like someone had removed every engine on every Model T in the area, and then put the engines back incorrectly.

"What a coincidence!" said Sparky.

"I think it's more than just a coincidence," Speed said. He turned to Mr. Clepto. "Let's go back to your house. I want to take a look at your old engine."

Up in Mr. Clepto's attic, Speed found the

original engine that had once been inside the Model T. The engine was covered in dust and grime.

He wondered why someone had been seeking out all the Model Ts in the area. There had to be something about the engines themselves.

That's when he saw it. Next to the engine's serial number was a code etched onto the steel.

Speed shone his flashlight on the engine so he could see it clearer.

The serial number started off normally: *9 8 7* . . . he wiped away more dust . . . *0 0 0 0*. Then there was a code carved in beside it.

Startled, Speed looked up at Mr. Clepto. "Do you think Light Fingers Clepto etched this code onto the engine?"

Mr. Clepto studied the code. Then, slowly, he nodded.

"I'm sure of it," he said. "Maybe my father was keeping something a secret . . . "

"Someone is trying to get ahold of this

engine," Speed said. "I wonder what this code means. It almost looks like map coordinates. I wonder . . ." He quickly memorized the code and hid the engine in the far back of the attic.

The code had to be coordinates. And someone wanted those coordinates badly.

But where did they lead?

Not too far away, in a secret hideout high in the mountains, Tongue Blaggard was waiting.

Blaggard's henchmen drove another Model T into the hideout. They popped open the hood and fiddled around inside, looking for something.

Blaggard stepped in to get the news. He stood there, menacingly, his arms crossed thickly over his chest, wanting to know what they found.

One of his henchmen approached. "Sorry, boss. This engine isn't the right one, either."

"That's funny," Blaggard said, though it was clear he didn't find this situation at all funny. "I wonder why we can't find the Model T with serial number 9870000. You'd think we would have found it by now."

"But . . . ," one of his henchmen started. "But, uh, boss, you sure you've got the number right? We've looked everywhere for it. And why, huh? You sure someone wasn't lying to you?"

The other henchmen cringed. Blaggard did not like to be questioned.

Blaggard scowled. "I say that's the right number so that's the right number," he blasted. "That story I heard in prison was not phony. I remember every word that old coot told me. Engine number 9870000 is the engine we want. Etched onto this engine is the code I need!"

Blaggard had spent more years than he wanted to count locked up in prison. His fellow prisoners were other crooks and thieves. One such criminal was Sammy Sluggem, the guy who

double-crossed the crook Light Fingers Clepto. No one had been able to take Light Fingers down until Sluggem got to him. But that was years and years ago. When Blaggard met Sluggem in prison, he was a grizzled old man with a shock of pure white hair and a chronic cough. Sluggem was never getting out of prison, not in his lifetime.

For some reason, Sluggem took a liking to Blaggard. Maybe he was lonely and wanted someone to tell his secrets to. Maybe he just wanted to hear himself talk. Either way, that's how Blaggard heard about the billion dollars that Light Fingers Clepto had supposedly hidden in Misty Valley. All Sluggem knew was that the way to find the loot was hidden somewhere on or inside a Model T car engine. Serial number 9870000 contained a code that would lead to a boulder under which the loot was buried.

Blaggard vowed that he'd bust out of prison and snatch that money for himself. That's what he told his henchmen. All he had to do was find that engine!

"I hope that story's true, boss," said one of his henchmen.

"Oh, it is," Blaggard said.

The radar screen started blinking.

"It looks like someone's nearby," another of his henchmen reported.

They went to the surveillance monitors that showed views of the mountain roads around the hideout. One showed motion.

Speeding up the narrow pass was a race car. It had a sleek white body and fender flares.

On the side of the car was a red circle with the number 5.

But that's not what caught Blaggard's attention—because the race car was flying a flag from its antenna. The flag read: *9870000*.

Blaggard got a smug look on his face. "It must be a trap," he said. "Someone knows we're looking for that engine. Go to your posts, men. Now's our chance."

Speed knew someone was looking for serial number 9870000, and he wasn't afraid to find out why.

So he and Mr. Clepto attached a flag to the antenna of the Mach 5 that clearly showed the engine's serial number. Then they drove through the area using the Mach 5 as bait. Speed knew it wouldn't be long before they were spotted.

Sure enough, when the Mach 5 came around a blind curve on the mountain road, a black car was waiting. Speed sped past it, and the black car began to follow.

Speed checked the rearview mirror. "They're falling for our trick," he said. "I knew they would."

Speed kept on driving, clouds of dirt from the unpaved mountain road billowing up behind him. The black car kept close on his tail.

"Hang on!" Speed shouted. He hit the accelerator, and the Mach 5 shot forward.

The driver in the black car tried to keep up.

70 mph . . . 80 mph . . . 90 mph . . . closing in on 100 mph.

Speed was testing the driver, pulling him along. And the roads on the mountaintop were no picnic. On one side of the car was a thick wall of craggy rock lifting straight up into the sky. The other side was the cliff edge. The road was separated from open air by only a guardrail.

Speed shot down the road. He drove through one curve and was coming up on another. This one was sharper, tighter.

"Uh-oh," he said.

Mr. Clepto held tightly to his seat.

Speed hit the gas and turned the wheel at the same moment. The Mach 5 stayed on the road, narrowly avoiding the guardrail that lined the cliff.

The black car wasn't so lucky.

It smashed head-on into the guardrail, almost flying off the cliff.

Speed had lost his tail.

But not for long—because coming up behind the crashed black car was another black car just like it.

It came around the bend and accelerated toward the Mach 5. It was gaining, getting closer and closer no matter how hard Speed hit the gas.

That's when Speed did the unexpected. He stomped on the brake. The Mach 5 came to a short stop in the middle of the mountain road.

The black car swerved, trying to avoid collision. But the driver of the black car had none of Speed's superior driving skills, and instead of coming to a smooth stop, he drove straight into the rock wall.

Crash. The black car was a pancake.

Speed heard a loud grinding noise in the sky up above. It was a giant cargo helicopter, heading straight for him. In his rearview mirror, Speed could see two more black cars and a truck.

"We'd better go!" Speed said.

Up above in the cargo helicopter, Blaggard communicated with his henchmen in the cars and truck below.

"There's just one car down there and no cops around, so let's get 'em," he commanded.

Following orders, the two black cars and the truck ganged up on Speed in the Mach 5. They came at him from both sides, trying to run him off the road.

Speed kept hold of the wheel and stayed on course. Mr. Clepto cowered in the passenger seat, the chase too much for him. But these thugs were no match for Speed Racer.

Or so he hoped.

Not far away, someone was on the way to help Speed. It was someone driving a yellow car with the number 9 on the doors: Racer X.

Racer X raced up the steep, rocky side of the cliff, not needing roads to make his way up the mountain. He took jumps and turns with ease. His skills made roads unnecessary.

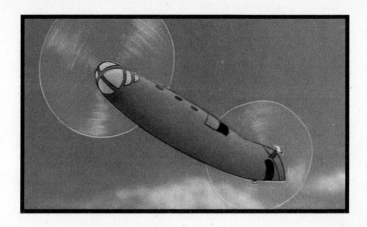

For the most part.

Racer X had driven up the side of the mountain straight up to . . . a narrow cliff.

He was stuck. And the Mach 5 could be seen speeding down the winding road far below— with a pack of cars chasing it.

How am I going to get down there in time? Racer X thought.

Just then, the cargo helicopter lowered a ramp. A legion of motorcyclists churned out onto the mountain road below.

The motorcycles hit the ground one by one by one, seemingly endless. And they were all

heading for the Mach 5.

When Speed saw the gang of motorcycles coming straight at him, he gasped. And in the rearview mirror, there were more black cars gaining on him. He was caught in the middle and, any second now, was about to collide with them.

It was time to make use of the powerful controls his father had designed on the Mach 5.

Speed pushed a button on the Mach 5's steering wheel control panel. The belt-tires activated. With his off-road wheels in place, Speed made a sharp turn and took the Mach 5 straight up the side of the mountain.

The cars and motorcycles didn't know what hit them. The white car had been there, and now it was gone. Speed was halfway up to the mountain peak before it occurred to them to look up.

Then they collided. The band of black cars smashed head-on into the motorcycles. The trucks knocked the cars off the road. The motorcycles flipped and knocked into one another.

It was a mess.

But Speed Racer and Mr. Clepto were in the Mach 5 on the other side of the mountain, out of harm's way.

Still, there were more cars coming up the mountain. Now Racer X had found his way off the cliff and down to the road. He spied the oncoming cars. *I've got to slow them down so Speed can get away,* he thought.

He was determined to cause a massive distraction.

Racer X shifted gears and hit the gas. His yellow race car hugged the curve so tightly that it rode up onto two wheels! He cut between the black cars, dodging them left and right with serious skill. Blaggard's henchmen didn't know how to handle him. They swerved, spun, tried to run him off the road, but no one could touch him. It was no wonder Racer X was known as one of the best racers in the world.

Racer X flew over the road. The drivers tried to follow him, but they just skidded off the road and into the rocks. A wrecked car burst into flames, closing the road from any further traffic.

Racer X looked back with satisfaction. *That'll keep them out of mischief for a while*, he thought.

Then he raced away, before Speed would know he'd been there.

◉　◉　◉　◉

Meanwhile, Speed saw his chance to get the information he was searching for. These cars and motorcycles that had been chasing him were sent by someone. And that someone wanted the engine. But who? And why?

Speed hid the Mach 5 around a blind bend and waited. One of the black cars had stalled out in the rocks and the driver was climbing out. Speed leaped out and grabbed the driver by the neck. He used a good wrestling choke hold that Pops, who had been a famous wrestler, had taught him.

"Now talk," Speed demanded. "Who told

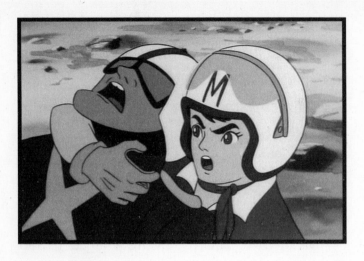

you to follow me?"

The driver wouldn't say.

"C'mon!" Speed demanded. "Who's behind this? Talk!"

The cargo helicopter rose up from the other side of the mountain, lowering itself directly over Speed. The propellers spun loudly in the wind.

Speed looked up. "I'll bet your boss is up there," he said to the driver.

Before the driver could respond, a voice boomed down from the helicopter. It was amplified, but Speed couldn't see who it was.

"You're right, sonny. Now let go of my man!" the voice demanded.

"Who are you?" Speed shouted.

Speed heard a sinister laugh. "Look behind you!" the voice warned.

Speed turned. All he saw was a gigantic man, a man bigger than any man he had ever seen. The man lifted one monstrous hand and brought it down hard on the back of Speed's neck.

Bam!

Speed dropped to the ground. He was out cold.

"Speed!"

Slowly, Speed opened his eyes. He thought he heard someone calling his name.

"Speed! Speed, wake up!"

Speed's vision was blurry, but he recognized the voice of Mr. Clepto, the old man he was trying to help.

Then Speed remembered everything. He remembered the Model T, the code on the engine, the chase on the mountain, being knocked out by a gigantic man . . .

"*Unnnngh,*" Speed groaned.

"This is a fine mess we're in, Speed," the old man said. He didn't look hurt, but he did look scared.

Speed rubbed his head and stood up. "Where are we?" he asked.

"Who knows. But I don't like it," Mr. Clepto said. "Just look around."

They were in a dim cave without an exit in sight. Torches were posted here and there, flickering patterns on the dark walls. It took Speed's eyes some moments to adjust to the light so he could see.

Sinister laughter echoed throughout the cave.

Speed looked up, up, up until there—in a hidden passageway that crossed over the cave—stood a man with a gleaming bald head. He wore a shiny suit and a nasty smirk.

He pointed a thick finger down at Mr. Clepto.

"Old man, you are the son of Light Fingers Clepto. Am I right?"

"How did you discover that?" Mr. Clepto asked.

"I've got a spy network throughout the world. I find out everything worth finding out."

Mr. Clepto shook his fist angrily. "You're nothing but a thief! You stole my precious Model T."

"I always get whatever I want. Now, tell me, what did you do with the original engine that was in the car?"

"Why should I tell you? What are you planning to do with it?"

"I don't plan to *do* anything with it. I just want to read the code on it because it'll tell me where a billion dollars was hidden in Misty Valley by your father."

"What?" Mr. Clepto said in confusion. "A billion dollars?!"

Speed listened in shock. He realized that the

code was indeed map coordinates: They would lead to the exact spot in Misty Valley where the money was buried.

"That's right," Blaggard said. "That's why I busted out of Songalong Prison, so I could get my hands on that loot. And you're gonna take me to it." He grinned.

Speed was shaking with anger. "You're the escaped convict Tongue Blaggard!" he shouted.

"Right," Blaggard said. "Now tell me where the real Model T engine is, or Tiny goes to work."

At the sound of his name, the gigantic man Speed had met briefly before stomped out from the shadows. He was so large, his head almost reached the ceiling of the cave. He advanced on Speed and Mr. Clepto.

Speed stood his ground. He couldn't let these criminals win.

But Speed was no match for the gigantic likes of Tiny.

In one single shove, Tiny knocked Speed off his feet and sent him flying to the other side of the cave.

"Force him to talk, Tiny!" Blaggard demanded. He was pointing at Mr. Clepto.

Tiny grabbed Mr. Clepto by the shirt. Mr. Clepto was just an old man—he looked like a small child in Tiny's grasp. He flailed around, but still, he sputtered, "I'll n-n-never tell you where that engine is, never!"

Tiny spoke in a low, rumbly voice. "Tell me." His enormous fist was raised. He was about to knock the helpless old man out.

Speed had to do something. "Don't hit him!" he cried out. "I'll tell you!"

"No, don't tell him anything, Speed!" Mr. Clepto cried.

"Tell us!" Blaggard shouted.

Speed was still on the ground, trying to catch his breath. He sat up and stared down Blaggard as best he could.

"The engine doesn't exist anymore," he lied. "I destroyed it."

Blaggard's eyes grew wide. "You destroyed it!"

"But I remember the code!" Speed cried.

Tiny let go of Mr. Clepto and went for Speed. He picked him up by the neck, about to toss him across the cave again.

"And I know the code is really map coordinates," Speed continued. "Let's go to Misty Valley right now. We can split the loot three ways. We'll be glad to share it. But if you won't agree to share, I won't tell you how to find the loot."

Without the exact coordinates, Blaggard would be searching under every stone in that valley for the rest of his life and he might never find the money.

Blaggard knew it, too. He might have been told that Light Fingers Clepto's money was buried under a boulder somewhere in Misty Valley, but he didn't have the slightest idea where to start digging. That's why he was so desperate for the engine's code.

"Think it over, Mr. Blaggard, think it over

carefully," Speed said. "Agree to share the money, and I'll agree to lead you to the spot in Misty Valley where it can be found."

"So you're not gonna tell me the code so I can find it myself?" Blaggard growled.

"No," Speed said. "You'll just have to take us with you."

Blaggard nodded for Tiny to let go of Speed. He left the cave to make his decision.

Mr. Clepto crept closer to Speed. "I wouldn't share anything with a man like that," he whispered.

"Shhh!" Speed whispered. Tiny was still in the cave with them, just waiting for the signal to pounce.

"Why did you say that?" Mr. Clepto whispered.

"I was just trying to save us from Tiny," Speed whispered. "If Blaggard needs us in order to find the money, he'll be sure not to hurt us. The first chance we get, we'll turn Blaggard over to the police and you'll be able to keep that billion for yourself."

"Well, the money did belong to my father, so I suppose it is now rightfully mine," Mr. Clepto said. "But I want to give you some of the money so you can enter the Multipeak Race."

"Shhh!" Speed warned again. Blaggard was coming back with his decision.

"I accept the deal, kid," Blaggard said. "You show us the way. And if the money's there where you say it is, we'll split the loot." Then he motioned for Tiny to carry them out of the cave.

☙   ☙   ☙   ☙

Back at the Racer house, dinner was about ready and Speed still wasn't home.

"It's late," Mom Racer said. "I wonder where he could be."

"I'm sure he's still training for the Multipeak Race," Pops said. "You know how much he wants to win that race."

Then the phone rang.

It was Speed!

He told Pops that he was staying over at a friend's house that night and wouldn't be home until tomorrow.

Pops said that was fine. He had no idea that Speed was making this phone call from deep inside a cave on top of a mountain. Or that Speed was using the telephone in Tongue Blaggard's headquarters, guarded by Blaggard and Blaggard's many henchmen, including the humongous Tiny.

Blaggard had told Speed to make this call to his parents to avoid any suspicion. "Good work, Speed," he said from behind Speed's back.

Still, this was Speed's one chance to let Pops know he needed help. But he had to do it in code, because everyone was listening.

"And Pops?" Speed added quickly. "Tell Trixie that the ring I wanted to get her cost six hundred and fifty dollars, so she may as well forget it. I'll have to get more money before I can afford it."

Blaggard and Tiny did not like this change in the planned conversation one bit.

Tiny forced him to hang up the phone.

But Speed had said all he'd needed to say. Once Trixie got that message about the $650 ring, she'd know it was a signal for help and that she should go looking for him. He just hoped she'd know where to go . . .

Blaggard insisted that they leave for Misty Valley right away. Speed and Mr. Clepto were allowed to drive in the Mach 5—but they were hemmed in by cars driven by Blaggard's henchmen.

"They're guarding us in the front and in the back," Mr. Clepto cried to Speed as they drove the highway. "We won't have the chance to call the police!"

"Don't worry," Speed said. "Once Pops tells Trixie about the ring, she'll know to start looking for us. Now I'll contact her on the radio."

Speed reached out to try the radio. By now, Trixie would have surely received his message, but she wouldn't know where to find him. He had to let her know they were heading to Misty Valley.

"Trixie! Trixie, come in!"

Speed heard only static.

"Wait!" Speed said. "I'm not getting a signal."

He opened the radio compartment to find a worrisome sight.

"Something's wrong," Speed said. "Some of the wires were cut."

Blaggard's men must have tampered with the radio—and unfortunately Speed couldn't fix it while driving. He'd have to wait until they were stopped somewhere and then try to reconnect the wires.

"Now I'm even more worried, Speed!"

Mr. Clepto cried. "My granddaughter and the children must be wondering where I am. This is a very dangerous adventure for an old man."

"Trixie will find a way to help us," Speed assured Mr. Clepto. "She always does."

"But I don't understand, Speed. Why would a ring that cost six hundred and fifty dollars mean anything different to Trixie?"

Speed tapped the Mach 5's dashboard.

"See the levels on the tachometer?" he said. "The tachometer measures the revolutions per minute in the engine. When this arrow goes over six hundred and fifty thousand, that means we're in the red zone. The engine is getting too hot. Danger. Trixie will know exactly what that means. She'll know that means we need help."

"Oh, I hope so, Speed, I hope so," Mr. Clepto said.

As they approached Misty Valley, the dirt roads turned red. In the valley was an active volcano—dark billowing smoke could be seen in the distance for miles. And the clay of the valley was deep red like nowhere else around, so all of Misty Valley looked like it was burned from staying out too long in the sun.

The drive through Misty Valley was longer than expected. When Blaggard heard that they wouldn't reach the spot until after midnight, when it would be too dark to look for the loot, he decided that they would stay the night in the first place they found.

This turned out to be a quiet lodge on a hillside. The police would never think to look for him there.

It was here, deep into the night, that Speed decided to try to fix the radio in the Mach 5. When the last of Blaggard's henchmen couldn't keep his eyes open and started snoring, Speed saw his chance. Slowly, he crept outside.

The Mach 5 was parked close by. Speed jumped inside and immediately opened the radio. If he could just reconnect the wires somehow, maybe he could pick up a signal . . .

He didn't have much time.

At that very moment, a snoring henchman jolted awake and leaped to attention inside the lodge. "Wake up!" he cried. "The kid slipped out!"

"What! Where'd he go?" the other henchmen yelled.

Blaggard stood up. "Let's find that kid," he growled.

Outside in the Mach 5, Speed had done fine work on the radio wires. He got a very faint signal. He couldn't reach Trixie, but he could try the police.

The radio crackled. "Hello! Hello! This is the police. Who's calling, and where?"

That's when the door to the lodge opened and Blaggard, Tiny, and the rest of the henchmen came out.

"Forget it," Speed said into the radio. He shut it down before Blaggard could see that he'd fixed it.

Blaggard approached. He leaned a heavy hand on the Mach 5's hood. "Checking to see if your car's all right?" he asked Speed. "You sure are attached to this car, aren't you?"

Speed tried to look innocent. "I, uh, yes," he said.

Blaggard shoved Speed aside into the passenger seat. Then he opened the door of the Mach 5 and sat down in the driver's seat.

"Hmmm," Blaggard said, having a look around inside the car. "The steering wheel's got a lot of buttons on it. Now what does this one here do?" He reached out a thick finger and shoved the button that read A.

The Mach 5 lifted off the ground.

"That's the automatic jack," Speed explained. "It raises the car several feet so it can be serviced."

Blaggard shrugged, unimpressed.

Out of the corner of his eye, Speed noticed gigantic Tiny standing in the shadows near the car, waiting to grab him if needed.

Blaggard ran his fingers over the remaining buttons on the steering wheel. "So which button's for the weapons?" he asked.

"Sorry," Speed said, though he wasn't sorry at all. "The Mach 5 doesn't carry any weapons. It was built for racing and that's it."

"Hmm," Blaggard said. "And what's this button here?" He lightly touched his finger to the G button.

The G Button!

Speed eyed it warily. He should have used that before Blaggard had a chance to come out.

"That's for a remote-control homing robot," Speed explained reluctantly. Maybe there would still be a chance for him to slip a message inside the robot and send it home . . .

Too late.

Blaggard pressed the G button. A robot built to look like a homing pigeon shot out of the Mach 5's hood.

A panel inside the Mach 5 opened up, and Blaggard leaned forward to inspect it. "Is this the remote control then?" he asked.

"Yes, but please don't fool around with it," Speed said quickly.

Blaggard ignored him. He wiggled the remote control left and right and up and down and around and around in wild circles. "It's like a toy airplane," he said.

Up above in the night sky, the flashing taillights on the homing robot could be seen zipping and zooming like a fighter pilot.

Blaggard was chuckling. "I haven't had this much fun since I was a kid!" he cried as he almost crashed the homing robot into a boulder.

Speed's heart was beating wildly. That homing robot was his last chance to contact home, and it was about to be smashed to pieces.

Blaggard pulled the remote controller down, and the homing robot touched ground, scuttling through the red dirt.

Speed's heart sank.

"What's this?" Blaggard said, nudging another control button labeled H. "Heh heh, I'll try it."

"Don't touch it!" Speed cried, unable to keep the panic from his voice.

Button H was the "home" button that would send the homing robot back to Speed's house. If Blaggard pressed it, Speed would never be able to send a message to Trixie!

Blaggard pushed the button. In one swift shot, the homing robot soared into the sky and vanished. Not even its taillights could be seen in the darkness.

"That homing robot can really fly!" Blaggard said, obviously delighted.

"Now it's gone," Speed said. He sat very still for a long moment, trying to think.

Blaggard just sent the homing robot back to my family, Speed thought. *But they won't know where I am. If only I'd been able to give the homing robot a message to carry . . .*

That same night at the Racer family home, Pops was woken by the doorbell. Blearily, he found his robe and slippers and went for the door. Outside was Speed's girlfriend, Trixie, and she was not happy.

"Speed was supposed to take me to a party tonight, but he stood me up!" Trixie cried angrily. "Where is he? I want to give him a piece of my mind."

That's when Pops remembered Speed's phone call. He looked down at his slippers, feeling a little embarrassed. "Uh, Trixie, there was something I forgot to tell you," he said. "Speed called this afternoon . . ."

"He called!" Trixie said. She lost her anger as Pops ushered her inside the house. She knew Pops didn't have the best memory when it came to anything other than automobiles. "What did he say, Pops?"

"He said he's spending the night at a friend's house," Pops said.

"What friend? Sparky?"

Pops shook his head. "I didn't ask," he admitted. Then his eyes lit up. "But I just remembered! He gave me a message for you. He said you should forget about that ring you wanted."

"Forget about what ring?" Trixie asked, thoroughly confused.

"He said it cost over six hundred and fifty dollars, so at least for now you should forget about it."

Trixie's eyes went wide. "Wait just a minute! He said six hundred and fifty, Pops? Are you sure?"

"Yes, I remember that exact number. Sure sounds expensive . . ."

"Pops!" Trixie cried. "He wasn't talking

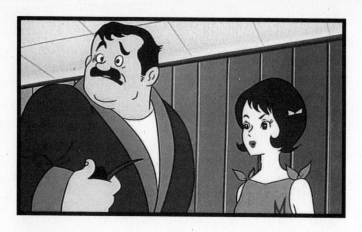

about any ring. Speed knows I wouldn't want him to buy me a ring when he's saving all his money to enter the Multipeak Race! That message was a code. Add a couple of zeros and it indicates the red zone of his tachometer. Speed's trying to tell me he's in danger!"

"Why . . . you're right," Pops said. "Why didn't I think of that?"

"Did he say anything else, Pops?"

A little shriek interrupted their conversation. "Mommy, I'm hungry!" came a voice from the kitchen. "I want a midnight snack!"

"Spritle," Mom Racer could be heard saying,

"what are you doing up at this hour?"

"The homing robot woke me up!" Spritle cried. "Can't I have some ice cream?"

Pops and Trixie shot to attention.

"The homing robot is here!" Pops said.

"Speed must have sent us a message," Trixie said.

They rushed into the kitchen to check the robot. Chim Chim was playing with it, tossing it up in the air. The robot was covered in streaks of red clay. Pops grabbed it from Chim Chim and opened it up.

"There's no note inside!" Trixie said, gasping. "Why would Speed send us the homing robot without a message inside?"

"Hmmm," Pops said, taking a closer look at the robot. "Look, there's red clay all over it," he said.

"Red clay!" Trixie said. She met Pops's eyes. They must have been thinking the same thing. "That could only mean—" Trixie started.

"Ice cream?" Spritle said hopefully. Chim Chim hooted wildly.

"No, not ice cream," Trixie said. "Speed needs our help. And I think we know where to find him . . ."

The next morning, Speed and Mr. Clepto were waiting to continue their journey deeper into Misty Valley. Blaggard's henchmen were guarding them nearby.

"I thought I heard a helicopter very late last night . . . Did you?" Speed whispered to Mr. Clepto.

"Uh-uh. I slept like a baby last night, or rather like an old man." He chuckled.

"Oh, well," Speed said, chuckling, too.

Still, Speed was sure he'd heard something that had sounded a lot like a helicopter. *Maybe that was Trixie's helicopter,* he thought. *Maybe she was out here searching for us.*

"Hey, boss!" one of the henchmen called out to Blaggard. Speed watched as the henchman walked up with a stranger. The henchman led the

girl over to Blaggard. "Look, we found a resident of Misty Valley."

Blaggard nodded his approval. "Good work," he said. "We can use her as a guide so we don't get lost."

"Why do you strangers want to go into Misty Valley?" the girl said. She had a strange accent.

"Just show us around and don't ask questions," the henchman said.

Speed watched from afar, frowning. Then he walked up to Blaggard, annoyed. "What do we need her for?" Speed said. "We can look for the buried money ourselves. I know where to find it.

I told you I have the coordinates."

"Do you think I trust you?" Blaggard snapped. "We're taking her along as backup."

"Fine," Speed mumbled.

"This kid will tell you the directions," the henchman said to the girl, pointing at Speed. "So you travel in the car with him."

The girl threw herself at Speed, obviously delighted. "I'm going to enjoy this trip!" she cried. "My name is Lana, and you're the most handsome boy I've seen in this valley."

Speed pushed her away.

Speed drove the Mach 5 to the spot in Misty Valley. In the car with him were Mr. Clepto, Lana, and one of Blaggard's men. Behind him were Blaggard's two cars.

Speed was worried enough about how he and Mr. Clepto would get away from Blaggard,

and now he also had to deal with Lana. She would not stop talking.

"Someday I want to move to the big city!" she said. "I would need someone to show me around. Ooh, I know! You can be my boyfriend and *you* can show me around, won't you?"

Speed cringed. "I have a girlfriend," he said. "I'm not interested."

"Well, the least I can do is show you some of the points of interest in Misty Valley," she said. She turned around in her seat and pointed into the trees. "Now look over there. That's a very important spot you must visit. See that little blue house in the distance? Hey, you're not looking!"

"I'm driving," Speed snapped.

"But *look*," Lana insisted.

Suddenly, with one swift push, she knocked the guard out of the Mach 5. He tumbled onto the road.

"Hey!" Speed cried. "Why'd you do that?"

"Now's your chance to get away!" Lana cried. "Hurry!"

"Why are you helping us?" Speed asked.

Lana winked and removed a wig that had been disguising her. She wiped off some makeup and there she was: Trixie!

Speed gasped. "I knew that helicopter I heard last night was you!" he cried. "Hang on!"

He shifted gears and floored the gas. The Mach 5 flew down the road, gaining distance on Blaggard's cars.

The Mach 5 squealed off the pavement and into the trees. There was no road through the woods, so the Mach 5 made one. Speed pressed a button on the steering wheel and saws shot out from the front of the car, cutting the brush and clearing a path as they went. Branches piled up behind them, blocking the way for any car that tried to come after them.

Blaggard and his men were left at the edge of the woods, unable to go in after Speed.

The Mach 5 emerged on the other side of the woods.

"They're not following us!" Trixie said.

"Of course not," said Speed. "But, Trixie, how in the world did you figure out where we were?"

"I saw the clay on the homing robot," she said. "Don't you know that Misty Valley is the only place this kind of red clay can be found?" She pointed toward the village in the distance. "C'mon," she said. "Pops is waiting for us in that blue house I showed you. We must get there, and fast!"

Soon enough, Speed, Trixie, and Mr. Clepto pulled up in front of the blue house. It was dead quiet. Speed walked straight up to the front door and walked in. Someone sat with his back to the door in a big chair.

"Pops!" Speed cried. "We're safe!"

"Pops, you can call the police now!" Trixie cried.

But when Pops turned around, he was not Pops!

It was Blaggard.

Speed gasped. "H-how did you—?" he started.

"My guard heard that impostor there talking about a blue house," Blaggard said, grinning menacingly at Trixie. "And here we are."

"Oh, no!" Trixie cried.

"Well, I'm glad you're back. I have a little surprise for you in there," Blaggard said. He pointed at a closed door. "Show 'em, Tiny."

Tiny stomped out from the next room and

opened the door. It was a closet. And inside was Pops, tied up and gagged. Pops struggled, trying to say he was sorry.

"Now, let's go get the loot," Blaggard said, pushing Speed, Trixie, and Mr. Clepto out the door. "Oh, and by the way, after this is all over, I'm keeping that helicopter."

Trixie's helicopter was waiting on the hillside, guarded by one of Blaggard's henchmen. Though the helicopter looked empty, it wasn't. Two little stowaways were hidden in the storage compartment under the seat. Quietly, Spritle and Chim Chim climbed out and hid in the bushes.

Soon, Speed had navigated everyone to the spot in Misty Valley where Light Fingers Clepto's loot was said to be buried. The place was a clearing hidden away far up in the hills. One of Blaggard's henchmen yelled from a far corner of the clearing. "Hey, boss! There's a big boulder back here."

Blaggard stomped over to the boulder in question to have a look. "Tiny, move the rock

aside," commanded Blaggard.

Tiny used all his weight to force the huge boulder a foot to the left. A hole was revealed beneath it. Blaggard nodded at Tiny, and Tiny shoved his giant arm down deep into the hole. Then he lifted out a briefcase.

Everyone gasped. Light Fingers Clepto really *had* hidden his money here!

"Open it up, Tiny!" Blaggard yelled.

Tiny knocked the lock off the briefcase with one hard punch. It came open easily.

Inside were stacks and stacks of hundred-dollar bills.

Everyone gasped louder than before. Mr. Clepto looked more shocked than anyone.

Blaggard turned to Mr. Clepto, a sinister grin on his face. "Take a good look at that billion dollars, Clepto. Because that's the last time you'll ever see it."

"What do you mean?" Mr. Clepto cried. "You're supposed to split it!"

"I'm getting rid of all of you," Blaggard said. "I don't want you going to the police. This loot belongs to me and only me."

Trixie put her hands on her hips and gave Blaggard a defiant look. "You don't deserve a penny of that money," she said.

"That's what you think," Blaggard said. "I deserve anything I can steal." Then he turned to his henchmen, who had formed a circle around Speed, Trixie, Pops, and Mr. Clepto. They were outnumbered at least five to one. "Get 'em, men," Blaggard growled.

The henchmen closed in.

We're done for, Speed thought.

Then rocks started raining down.

"We're under attack!" one of Blaggard's men cried.

"They're on the hill!" another man cried.

Rocks came from all directions. An army of monkeys was jumping up and down on the hill. They were pitching rocks and stones at the henchmen, knocking them out one by one.

Speed looked up at the monkeys. He saw a familiar face.

"Chim Chim's the leader!" he cried.

Sure enough, there was Chim Chim, hooting

in excitement. And Spritle was there beside him, throwing a few rocks of his own.

Blaggard's men were no match for them.

"Who said a barrel of monkeys was fun?!" cried a henchman as some of the monkeys ganged up on him, knocking him to the ground.

Blaggard stumbled out of the hail of rocks. He had his sights set on Chim Chim. "I'll get that monkey," he growled, but before he could do anything of the sort, Spritle swung over on a vine and knocked him in the head with a sharp kick.

"Spritle, what are you doing here!" Pops shouted.

Blaggard was on his knees, dazed.

Spritle swung back and forth. "Pops, show me what a good wrestler you are!"

"Good idea, Spritle," Pops said. "I almost forgot that I used to be a champ." Pops turned. He found Speed and Trixie fighting off attackers.

Off to the side, Blaggard was getting up, unguarded.

"The boss is mine!" Pops hollered. He took a running leap toward Blaggard, catching him in a headlock and knocking him flat on his back. "That's just the beginning," Pops said.

But a henchman climbed up Pops's back.

"Throw him off, Pops!" cried Trixie.

Pops twisted around and got the henchman by the shoulders. Then he lifted him up high in the air and pitched him into the dirt. He threw another henchman at a boulder and another at the side of the mountain.

Nearby, Speed and Trixie used their martial arts skills to defend themselves.

Then Tiny advanced on Speed. He threw a chop. Speed ducked out of the way. He threw a punch. Speed jumped to the side. Tiny got mad, madder than before, and geared up all his strength. Speed tried to catch his breath. Tiny was coming at him with both enormous arms outstretched.

"Don't worry, Speed!" Spritle cried. "I'll take care of him." He shot a well-aimed rock at Tiny. It hit Tiny square between the eyes, dazing him for a moment.

The moment was long enough for Speed to get his bearings. Tiny grabbed for him, but Speed was fast and rolled him in a wrestling move he'd

learned from Pops. He slammed Tiny hard into the pile of rocks. There was a low rumble, and the rocks came loose. A cavern opened up beneath them, and Tiny fell into it.

"Good work," Pops said. "That takes care of him."

Trixie, Mr. Clepto, and Spritle joined Speed and Pops. They cheered.

"There aren't many more left," Pops said. But he spoke too soon.

Blaggard was back. He stood on a hill above them, a gigantic boulder pointed straight at them. "All I have to do is let go, and you'll all be knocked off that cliff," he called down.

Speed took a quick look around. He realized that during the mayhem they had come to a cliff, and they were very close to the edge. The fall was dangerous and far. He knew no one would survive it.

How will we get out of this?! Speed thought wildly.

Speed and the gang were backed up to the edge of the cliff, nowhere to run. All Blaggard had to do was let go of the boulder he was holding, and they were done for.

Then an engine sounded, and a yellow race car was flying straight at Blaggard. The race car chased him off the hill and knocked the boulder out of harm's way. The car skidded to a stop before Speed.

"Racer X!" Speed cried in surprise. "You got

here at just the right moment!"

Racer X, his identity hidden behind his mask, gave Speed a nod.

Off to the side, Blaggard crawled to his knees. When no one was looking, he snatched the briefcase with the loot in it and ran for his car.

Speed didn't notice until he saw Blaggard's car peel away in a cloud of red dirt.

Speed thought fast. He did a running leap into the Mach 5, starting the engine in a matter of seconds—just like he'd learned on the racetrack from Fireball Rust.

The Mach 5 set its sights on Blaggard's black car and was in hot pursuit. Speed jammed the gas, gaining on Blaggard. The chase took a turn off the mountainside and onto the paved roads.

Blaggard hit a button and let out some oil onto the road, hoping that the Mach 5 would skid off the side of the mountain.

The Mach 5 hit the oil slick and did a 360, narrowly missing the guardrail. Speed cried out and activated the belt-tires. The Mach 5 righted itself, moving swiftly over the pavement without another mishap.

Inside the black car, Blaggard was sweating. "Huh," he said. "Let's see him get out of this." He pressed a button that spilled gasoline onto the road. Then he lit the tail flames. Flames broke out, setting the pavement on fire.

Seeing that, Speed pressed another button on his steering wheel. The Mach 5 swiftly moved through the wall of flames as if it were nothing.

Blaggard groaned. "Fire doesn't have any

effect on that car," he muttered. "Let's try water."
He turned off the road into the lake. His car was equipped with aquatic propellers. It shot through the water without sinking.

The Mach 5 followed. It hit the water, bounced a few times, and sunk.

Blaggard glanced in his rearview—nothing appeared to be following him. He chuckled.

Little did he know it, but the Mach 5 had been built to withstand all of the elements. The Mach 5 was merely speeding out of sight underwater, like a submarine.

Blaggard reached the shore of the lake and

slowed, thinking he was safe. But the Mach 5 shot out from the depths of the lake, speeding up behind him.

Blaggard growled in frustration and headed back for the roadway. "Send the helicopter," he radioed. "I'm still being chased by that kid."

Just then, the Mach 5 blasted around him and cut him off. Speed jumped out and yelled in Blaggard's direction. "Get out, Blaggard!"

Blaggard opened his door and stepped out onto the pavement. He held the briefcase full of money tight in his grasp.

But before Speed could make a move for the briefcase, a helicopter appeared in the sky and lowered a rope ladder for Blaggard to grab on to. Blaggard started climbing. "So long!" he called down to Speed.

Speed hit a button. During the previous night, Trixie had returned the homing robot to the car, and now Speed had one last chance to use it. The homing robot shot upward, and Speed used the controller to direct it at Blaggard, who was still swinging from the rope ladder in the sky.

With one swift jab, the homing robot knocked the briefcase out of Blaggard's hand.

It fell, knocking against rocks and boulders and thumping clumsily down the side of the mountain. Blaggard jumped off the ladder, trying to follow. But when the briefcase landed, it broke open. The money they had seen just minutes before started to disintegrate. Blaggard stumbled and crawled for it, but by the time he reached it, the loot he'd wanted so badly had turned to dust.

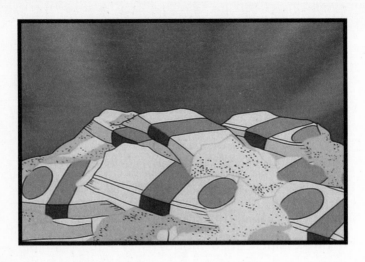

"What happened?!" he cried.

Speed stepped up. "It must be because the money was buried in volcanic ground for so many years," he said. "Maybe because of that, it deteriorated . . ." He shrugged.

Blaggard was stunned. He started sobbing as the wind picked up the last of the money dust and carried it away.

Soon enough, the police arrived. They had received Speed's radio signal from the day before. Now they had Blaggard in handcuffs. Inspector Detector, the head of the police unit, was very pleased by the capture of the escaped convict.

But one person was not happy. "What happened to all the money my father left me?" Mr. Clepto cried. "Where's the billion dollars?"

"It all turned to dust and blew away," Speed explained.

Mr. Clepto put his head in his hands.

Speed frowned. He wished it could have gone another way.

Pops put his hand on Speed's shoulder. "Don't feel so bad, Speed," he said. "Inspector Detector has something to say."

Inspector Detector held out his hand to Speed. "First of all, congratulations, Speed Racer."

Speed shook the inspector's hand.

The inspector wasn't finished. "Speed, you were instrumental in the capture of one of the world's most dangerous criminals," he said. "And for that, we are most grateful. You will receive a reward of one hundred thousand dollars."

Speed's eyes went wide. "Oh!" was all he could say.

Trixie leaped to his side, grabbing him in a giant hug. "Speed!" she cried. "Now you have more than enough money to enter the Multipeak Race! Isn't that wonderful?"

The sound of an engine could be heard

coming up the hill. It sputtered and chugged along. It could only be . . .

Mr. Clepto's Model T! It pulled up, filled to the brim with Mr. Clepto's granddaughter and the adopted children. "Grandpa!" Susie cried. "We were so worried about you!" Susie and the kids jumped out of the antique car and into Mr. Clepto's arms.

Speed took this in, an idea forming.

"Now, don't worry, children," Speed overheard Mr. Clepto saying. "Even though I didn't get that money, we'll make out all right.

Who needs money when you have such a wonderful family?"

Speed smiled. He had made his decision.

"You know what?" he said. "I'm going to give my reward money to Mr. Clepto to help him take care of all his adopted children."

"But what about the Multipeak Race, Speed?" Pops asked.

"Some things are just more important," Speed said.

"You're right," Pops said, watching Mr. Clepto and the children. He began to tear up. "Speed, you are absolutely right."

Knowing he had done the best thing, Speed waved as Mr. Clepto and his children drove away out of Misty Valley. It was thanks to Speed, Trixie, Spritle, Chim Chim, and Pops—and even Racer X—that Mr. Clepto would be able to provide for his family. To Speed, this felt even better than crossing the finish line first at the toughest race in the world.

I sure had a tough time with those twisty mountain roads near Blaggard's hideout. There were a few times I thought the Mach 5 would be run off the cliff, but I kept my eye on the road and held tight to the curves—and somehow I stayed on track.

But you know what? Those mountain roads were nothing compared to the time I joined some of the greatest race car drivers in the world on a racecourse with the seven swiftest turns ever set to pavement.

That course was called the Snake Track . . . and, believe me, it sure earned its name. Want to know how I made it around those turns? Want to know if the Mach 5 crossed the finish line first? Just read on!

The Snake Track
Part One: The Course

Speed Racer first spotted the Snake Track while flying high in Trixie's helicopter. From up above, the racetrack looked like a long snake, slithering this way and that from start to finish. In fact, the Snake Track had more sharp turns than any other racecourse the world over: seven sharp curves altogether. This track was where Speed's next race—the Super Car Race—was going to be held.

Speed gazed out of the helicopter warily. Trixie had taken Speed and Sparky up into the sky for a sneak peek at the course, just to get an idea of what Speed was in for. Speed had entered the Mach 5 in the race and, just three days later, he would be gearing up to drive his best against some of the most skilled drivers in the racing industry.

Speed swallowed, getting nervous. The

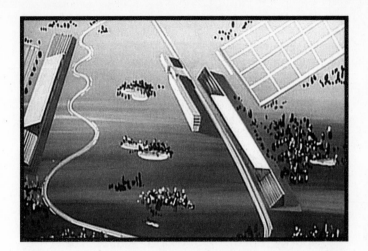

Snake Track was a long run of tightly twisting turns—more turns than Speed had ever seen on a professional course before. He had no idea how cars would be able to drive at top speed around those turns without crashing or running head-on into the walls.

"I can't believe they're actually holding the Super Car Race here," Trixie said. "They've never had the Super Car Race on a course like that before."

Speed just nodded without answering.

"I mean, it looks like a really tough race to win, doesn't it, Speed?" Trixie said.

"It looks dangerous," Sparky added. He was gazing down at the track as the helicopter swept closer to it, a look of concern on his face. "All those turns, one right after the other. I mean, you sure know how to maneuver the Mach 5, Speed, but with those turns, you could lose control!"

Sparky and Trixie didn't realize that they were only making Speed more nervous about the upcoming race by talking like this.

"I know," Speed said quietly. "Every curve on that track is going to be tough. It'll take all

the experience and skill I have to win."

"Yeah, and a tremendous amount of luck," Sparky mumbled.

I've got to try out those curves so I don't crash, Speed thought with alarm. The Super Car Race was the biggest race he'd ever been in. He didn't want to make a fool of himself in front of professional race car drivers from all over the world. And he sure didn't want to wreck the Mach 5.

He turned to Trixie and Sparky. "Hey, do you think we could take the Mach 5 here tomorrow so I could do some practice runs on the track before the big race?"

"Like try out those turns on the Snake Track?" Sparky said. "Good idea!"

"Yeah, great idea, Speed," Trixie said.

"I'll need a lot of practice," Speed said. *More than a lot,* he thought.

And that sure was the case. The next day,

Speed was poised in the Mach 5, ready to hit the course for the first time. The big race was two days away.

Trixie, Spritle, and Chim Chim were on the sidelines, watching. Sparky had the hood of the Mach 5 open and was doing one final tune-up to the engine.

"There we go," he said, and closed the hood. "You ready to try out those turns, Speed?"

Speed had the whole course to himself. No other drivers were practicing that afternoon. He lowered his driving visor and focused his eyes on the curve up ahead. All he could see in front of him was the first turn. That turn was so sharp, he wasn't sure which way the course went after it. He'd just have to practice, practice, practice to get through this race.

"I said . . . are you ready?" Sparky called to Speed.

"I'm ready," Speed said. He shifted into gear,

jammed the gas, and was off!

The Mach 5 tore over the asphalt. At the first turn, Speed steered to the left, but the turn was so sharp, sharper than he expected, that he had to downshift to stay in the lane. He kept going. When he came to the next turn—it was there, sooner than he'd expected—he had to downshift again. Each time he downshifted, the Mach 5 slowed, losing valuable time. It was that way around all of the Snake Track's seven curves. When Speed reached the finish line and Sparky showed him his final time, he knew there was no

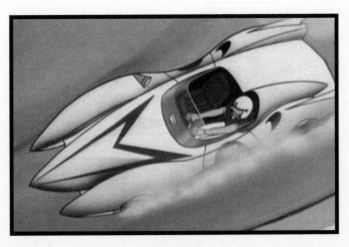

way he'd win the Super Car Race at that pace.

"I'm going too slow," Speed said.

Sparky shrugged. "But you don't want to crash," he said. "Then you'd be out of the race for good. The other drivers will have to go slower, too."

Speed shook his head. "Those racers are serious professionals. They'll know how to handle these curves. I've got to do better."

He thought for a moment.

"My timing's no good," he said at last. "My technique just isn't working."

"What else can you do, Speed?" Sparky asked.

"I'm going to try those curves without downshifting," Speed said. "I can't slow down, no matter how sharp the turn is. Going slow is no way to win the race."

"But driving like that is risky!" Sparky cried.

"I have to try," Speed said. He put his driving

visor back on and motioned for Sparky to move out of the way.

Then Speed stepped down hard on the Mach 5's accelerator, launching it forward and back onto the course.

As he approached the Snake Track's first curve, he quickly turned the steering wheel but still kept his foot on the gas. He didn't downshift. He didn't touch the brake, not even a little. He kept turning the wheel, trying to stay in the lane. But the turn was too tight for him, and he was

going too fast to double back. All of a sudden he lost control. The Mach 5 flipped upside down and skidded wildly across the track!

Spritle, Trixie, Sparky, and Chim Chim ran down the track to see if Speed was all right.

Fortunately, he was. Speed crawled out unharmed from beneath the overturned Mach 5.

"Speed, you haven't been hurt!" Trixie cried with relief.

"Maybe you shouldn't do this race, Speed," Sparky said. "It's too dangerous."

But Speed shook his head. He was determined to find a way around that Snake Track, no matter what. "Is the Mach 5 okay?" he asked. "As long as the Mach 5 is okay, I'm doing that race."

Part Two: The Technique

Sparky was able to repair the Mach 5 for the Super Car Race without any trouble. The next day, just one day away from Speed's real debut on the Snake Track, Trixie tried to take Speed out driving so he'd relax a little. They had the top of the Mach 5 down and were cruising slowly through the countryside.

Speed couldn't stop thinking about the Snake Track. He knew he needed a new technique in order to get quickly around those turns without crashing. He just had no idea what it could be.

Suddenly, a red race car sped past, followed closely by two black cars. The two black cars were chasing the red one, trying to wreck it. But,

amazingly, when one of the black cars tried to ram into it, the driver of the red car maneuvered up onto two wheels to evade the attack! The black car missed its target completely.

"Oh, Speed, did you see that?" Trixie cried.

The red car sped forward, still driving on only its two right tires.

Speed followed the chase in the Mach 5. When the black cars came at the red race car again, the red car tilted to the left this time.

Somehow the driver was able to drive it while balancing on only the tires on the left side.

It was incredible! Only a professional race car driver could pull off a trick like that.

Taking curves on just two wheels . . . that's the technique I've got to use! Speed thought excitedly.

But right now the red car was in trouble, and Speed wanted to help. He wasn't sure why the black cars were chasing it, but anyone who drove with that kind of skill was someone he wanted to talk to. He couldn't let a phenomenal driver like that get hurt!

Speed released the Mach 5's homing pigeon and steered it at the two pursuing cars, running them off the road one at a time.

The red car slowed to a stop, and Speed pulled up beside it.

"Are you okay?" Trixie called over to the driver of the red car.

"I'm fine," the man answered, though he seemed a little shaken.

"Why were those cars chasing you?" Trixie asked. "I'm Trixie, by the way, and that's Speed."

"And I'm Rock Force," the man said. "Those cars must have been from a rival racing team. They've been threatening me for weeks, ever since they heard I'm driving in the Super Car Race tomorrow. They know I've got a good shot to win."

"I knew it!" Speed cried out. "I *knew* you were a race car driver! Somehow you managed to drive on only two wheels, and you never lost control. And at the same time, you didn't slow down one bit . . . you didn't downshift, did you?"

"No . . . ," the man said. "Why do you ask?" He had a strange smile on his face as he looked the Mach 5 over. "Are you driving in the Super Car Race tomorrow, too?"

"Yes, I am," Speed admitted.

"And you're curious about my technique because you've seen those killer turns at the Snake Track, haven't you?" Rock Force continued.

"Speed's been having trouble with those turns," Trixie said.

"Trixie!" Speed said. "Don't tell him that!"

But Rock Force seemed nice enough. "Just because there are some people who don't want me in that race doesn't mean I'd keep anyone from racing against me . . . ," he said. "Even if they happened to borrow my technique." Then he winked at Speed.

Speed jumped. Was Rock Force saying he wouldn't mind if Speed tried his technique against him? "But, Mr. Force—" Speed started.

Rock Force wouldn't let him finish. "Thanks for helping me out back there," he said. "See you on the Snake Track tomorrow, kid." Then, quickly, without another word, he drove away.

For the rest of the night, Speed practiced the new technique of taking the Mach 5 up onto

two wheels to maneuver around sharp turns. It was difficult at first, but little by little he gained confidence and was able to do the technique successfully—most of the time. Even though he hadn't yet mastered it, he was determined to try it out at the Super Car Race.

Part Three: The Showdown

The day of the Super Car Race, Speed was at the starting line in the Mach 5, mentally preparing himself. He navigated the course in his head over and over but was still a little nervous about trying the new technique without having practiced it more. Soon enough, a car he recognized pulled up: the red race car driven by Rock Force.

Rock and Speed nodded at each other.

The roar of the engines echoed throughout the stadium as the drivers readied themselves for the start of the race.

After a few moments of preparation, it was

time. Speed took a deep breath and lowered the visor on his racing helmet.

The racing official waved the green flag to start the race, and in one thunderous movement the race cars shot forward.

The Mach 5's engine roared as Speed blasted it past the other race cars on the first straightaway. The Mach 5 had taken the lead! Rock Force's red car followed closely behind in second place.

At the first curve, Speed hesitated. Suddenly unsure of using the new two-wheel technique, he downshifted the Mach 5 and decelerated to safely take the turn. A mistake. Rock Force took his race car up onto two wheels, slipping right past the Mach 5 and pulling into the lead.

The Snake Track was turning out to be even trickier than the drivers had imagined. Many of the other drivers were not as lucky as Speed or Rock. Some of their cars slid off the track entirely. One car after the other smashed into the walls and into one another, unable to safely maneuver past the very first turn. It was a mess!

Rock and Speed maintained their lead. Speed took great advantage of the second straightway and caught up to Rock's car. At the second curve, Rock maneuvered his car up onto two wheels, and, without hesitation, Speed did the same. Both cars zipped around the curve on two wheels, astonishing the crowd!

But toward the end of the curve Speed nearly lost control of the Mach 5 and had to take

it back down to four wheels to prevent himself from flipping over.

What a close call! Speed thought. *I just didn't have enough time to practice the new technique. I'd better not try that again or I'll surely crash.*

More of the other race cars lost control around the second turn. Now only a few racers remained. Rock maintained his lead, but Speed was right on his tail.

I'm just going to have to beat him on each of the straightaways, Speed thought. He slammed the Mach 5's accelerator down to the floor and shot past Rock's red race car!

The Mach 5's engine hummed as Speed took the lead again.

Speed's and Rock's race cars went on like this throughout the entire course. Rock would take the lead at each of the curves, and Speed would move past him at each of the straightaways.

At the seventh and final curve of the Snake Track, only Speed and Rock were left in the race. All the other race cars had either slid off the course, crashed into the wall, or stalled out.

Rock once again took the lead around the curve, but the last stretch of the course before the finish line was a straightaway and Speed was quickly catching up.

"Go!" shouted Sparky and Trixie.

"Pass him, Speed! Pass him!" Spritle shouted as the two cars neared the finish line.

Speed and Rock were dead even. Speed pulled ahead, then Rock pulled ahead, and they

went back and forth like this all the way past the checkered flag.

The crowd cheered loudly as the two race cars zipped past the finish line.

It was clearly going to be a close race to call, but after a few minutes, the announcer shouted over the loudspeaker, "Rock Force wins!"

The announcer continued, "Both racers crossed the finish line at almost the same instant, but Rock won by a hair and gets the trophy!"

Minutes later, Rock and Speed stood proudly

atop the winner's podium, in first and second places respectively.

"Congratulations, Mr. Force. You're an incredible driver," Speed said.

Rock smiled and patted Speed on the shoulder. "With a little more practice, Speed, I'm sure you'll have no trouble using my technique in the next race," he said.

"I *will* practice, and I'll win the next race," Speed replied, grinning. He'd made use of a new technique, but more than that, he'd conquered his fear of the Snake Track and stayed in the race until the very end.

"Oh, I think I'll win the next race," Rock said with a chuckle.

"Just you wait, Mr. Force," Speed said. "I'm never going to stop practicing, no matter how tough the next race turns out to be!"